Mo Smells the Ballpark

written by
Margaret Hyde
with Nichelle Robinson

illustrated by
Aman Chaudhary

Sky Pony Press
New York

This book is dedicated to Frank Robinson, an amazing father and living legend. And to everyone who loves baseball, especially Jackson Marcum, whose kindness inspires me every day. A special thanks to Major League Baseball for their support and belief in this book.

Sky Pony Press books may be purchased in bulk at special discounts for sales promotion, corporate gifts, fund-raising, or educational purposes. Special editions can also be created to specifications. For details, contact the Special Sales Department, Sky Pony Press, 307 West 36th Street, 11th Floor, New York, NY 10018 or info@skyhorsepublishing.com.

Sky Pony® is a registered trademark of Skyhorse Publishing, Inc.®, a Delaware corporation.

Visit our website at www.skyponypress.com.

10 9 8 7 6 5 4 3 2 1

Manufactured in China, January 2014
This product conforms to CPSIA 2008

Library of Congress Cataloging-in-Publication Data

Hyde, Margaret E.
 Mo smells the ballpark / written by Margaret Hyde ; illustrated by Aman Chaudhary.
    pages cm
 Summary: "Mo attends the Bark in the Park day at the ballpark and quickly learns that it's not about winning but rather how you play the game"—Provided by publisher.
 ISBN 978-1-62873-668-7 (hardback)
 [1. Dogs--Fiction. 2. Baseball--Fiction. 3. Smell--Fiction.] I. Chaudhary, Aman, illustrator. II. Title.
 PZ7.H9679Mo 2014
 [E]--dc23
                        2013035907

Book design and production by Sara Kitchen

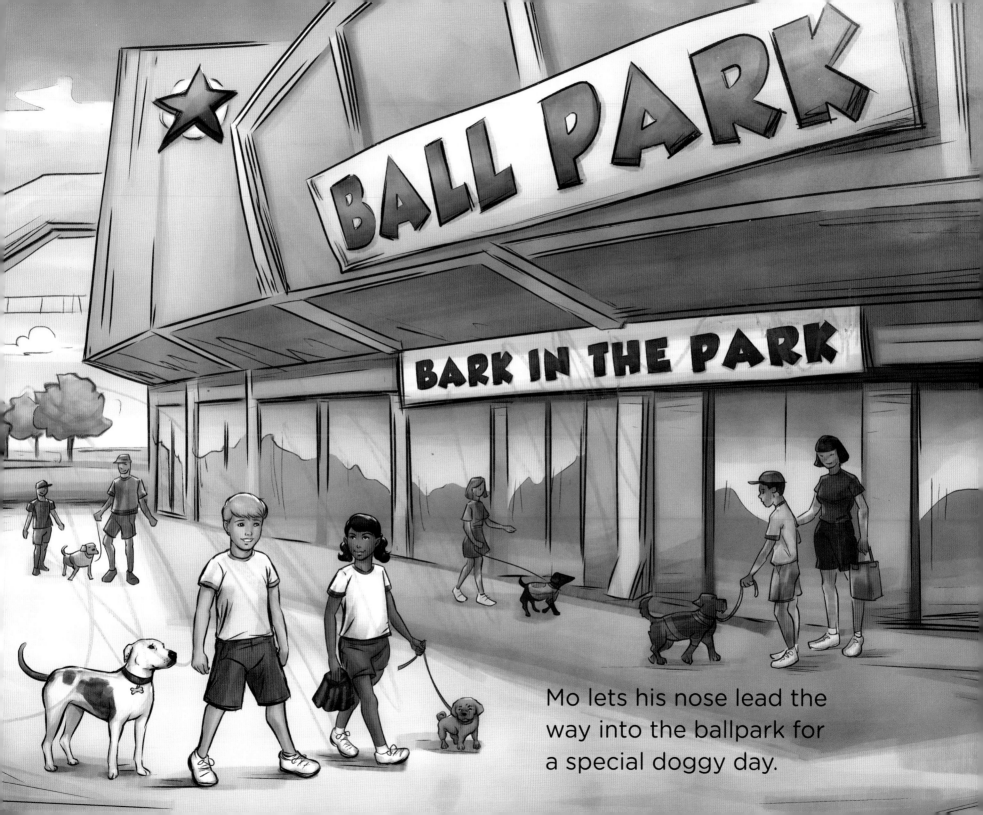

Mo lets his nose lead the way into the ballpark for a special doggy day.

Mo smells baseball everywhere—
leather gloves, wooden bats, peanuts,
and cracker jack.

Inside, Jasper and Molly gaze up at
the giant scoreboard lit up in the sky.

Down on the field, a doggy parade is about to begin. Major League players are warming up. As they pass, one player gives Mo a pat and signs Jasper's hat.

Mo's puppy pal, Lucky, anxiously eyes the baseballs sailing by.

Oh, no! The leash slips from Molly's hand and Lucky darts onto the field.
   In the dugout all the players laugh and shout, "Go, pup, go!"

Mo is on the field in a flash, trying to get Lucky back. But the smell of the fresh cut grass and the sight of home plate take him into a baseball daydream.

Mo suddenly hears the umpire shout: "Play ball!"

Molly is Team Mo's ace
pitcher. She is determined to
get a no-hitter against the
Big Dogs baseball team.
Molly takes the mound.

One . . . Two . . . Three Strikes! Molly gets the Big Dogs Team out.

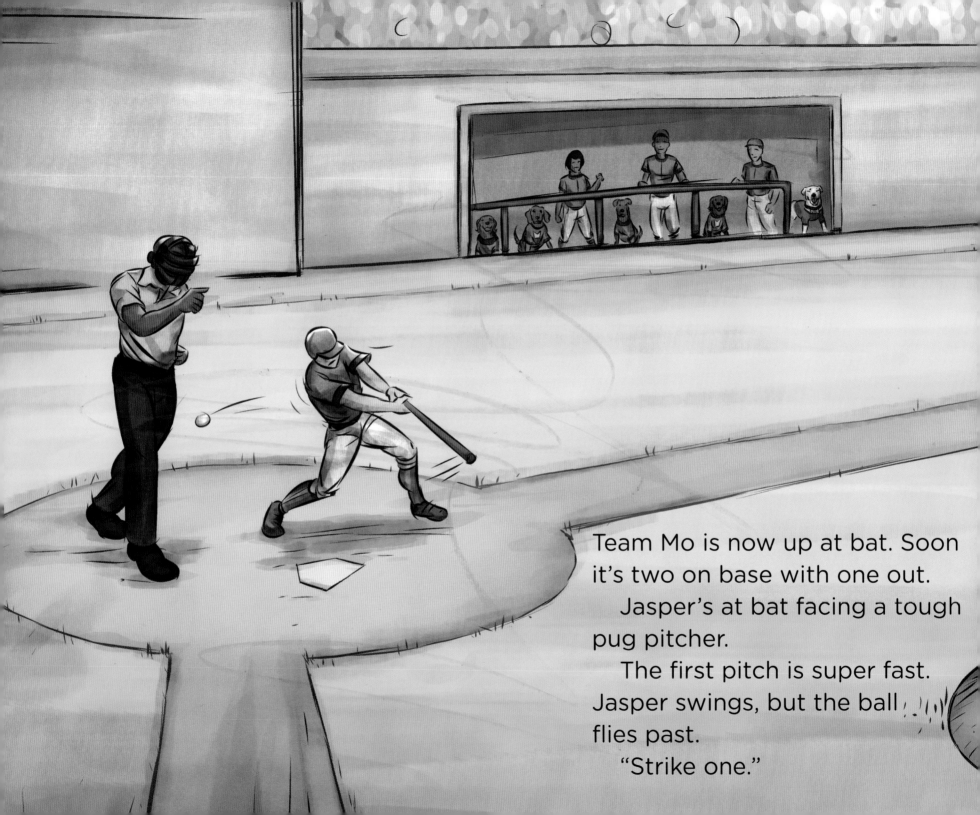

Team Mo is now up at bat. Soon it's two on base with one out.

Jasper's at bat facing a tough pug pitcher.

The first pitch is super fast. Jasper swings, but the ball flies past.

"Strike one."

Molly and Mo cheer Jasper on. They know he can do it.

The next pitch is way too low.
Jasper swings and the ump
shouts, "Strike two!"
   Jasper knows he needs to hit
the ball and follow through.

On the next pitch, Jasper hits the ball with a thunderous whack! It's a fly ball! He takes a deep breath as the crowd roars.

The right fielder jumps up and catches it in her mouth.

"You're out!" the ump calls. Jasper sulks back to the dugout with his head low.

Knowing Jasper feels bad,
Mo goes and nuzzles his hand.
   He cheers him up, the way
only a best friend can.
   Jasper hugs Mo and gives
him the bat.
   "Mo, it is up to you. Show
them what our team can do."

Mo sniffs home plate then bites his bat.
The Big Dog pitcher throws a surprise
knuckle ball that zigzags and falls.
Mo tries to bunt, but it's a miss. Strike
one for Mo, but he is still having fun.

The next pitch is a little high.
Oh, no! Mo swings and the whole crowd sighs.
Strike Two.
Mo will try again for himself, his team, and the win.
He doesn't want to let them down.

The pitch is perfect—right to Mo.
    The ball connects with the sweet spot
on his bat and soars over the fence.
    It's a home run!

"Three cheers for Team Mo!" They worked together and had lots of fun! Mo slides into home and Team Mo runs out to celebrate.

The roar of the crowd, the barking dogs, and the smell of a delicious hot dog awaken Mo from his daydream. He grabs Lucky's leash and they head back to the stands.

It is the seventh-inning stretch.
Jasper and Molly sing "Take Me Out to the Ball Game" with the crowd.
Mo and Lucky howl in tune.
For it's root, root, and root for Mo's Team.

It's all for one and one for all. Mo and his friends love baseball.